Hairy HAROLD

Laurence Anholt

Illustrated by Tony Ross

ORCHARD

www.anholt.co.uk

Hee, hee, hello everyone!
My name is **Ruby** and I have the
funniest family in the world.
In these books, I will introduce you
to my **freaky family**.

You will meet people like…

But this book is all about...my
hairy uncle, **HAROLD**.

We are going to meet my uncle,
Harold, the hairiest man in the
WHOLE UNIVERSE. Nobody is
hairier than Harold.

Uncle Harold is proud of the way he looks. Uncle Harold has a big mirror so that he can see all his beautiful hair.

Uncle Harold has a shelf covered with brushes and combs and bottles of shampoo.

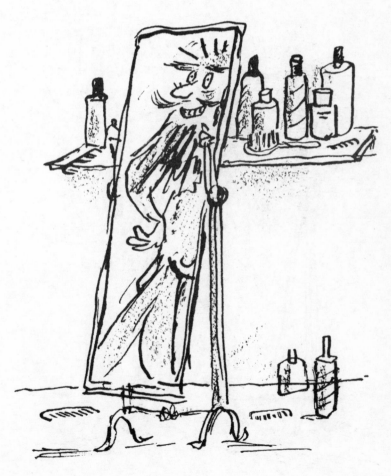

Every morning, my hairy uncle Harold stands in front of his big mirror and says, "Hello, Harold, you lovely big hairy man."

Then Harold brushes his big
bushy beard.

And Harold curls his twisty
moustache.

And Harold washes his beautiful
long hair.

It takes a very long time. Because
Harold has hairs in his nose.

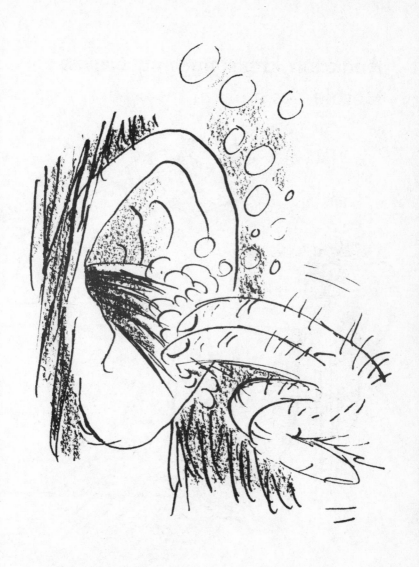

And Harold has hairs in his ears.

And Harold has huge eyebrows.

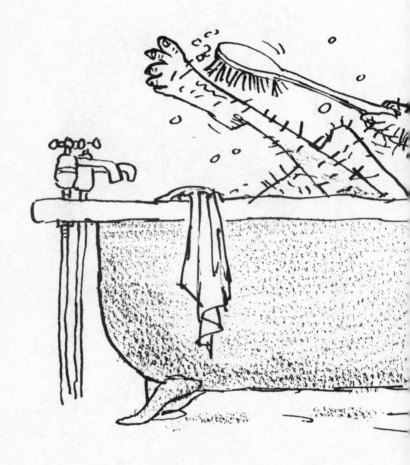

And Harold has hairy legs.

And Harold has hairy hands.
And Harold has hairs on his chest,
his knees, his neck, his nose.

Harold has hairs on his elbows, his belly, his back, his toes.

One day, my uncle Harold went
for a walk. He walked past a
shop. A beautiful woman was
working inside.

"Hello, Harold, you lovely big hairy man," she called.

Harold and the woman fell in love. The woman was a famous hairdresser. Her name was Shirley.

Uncle Harold loved Shirley's shop because it was full of big mirrors and lots of combs and brushes.

Shirley loved Harold's hair. She
liked to practise all the latest styles.

Everyone who passed the shop
wanted Shirley to do their hair too.
"We want beautiful hair just like
Harold," they said.

Harold had a side parting.

Everyone wanted a side parting.

Harold had a centre parting.

Everyone wanted a centre parting.

Harold had his hair brushed back.

Everyone wanted their hair
brushed back.

Harold had his hair
brushed forward.

Everyone wanted their hair
brushed forward.

Harold had a spiky mohican.

Everyone wanted a spiky mohican.

Uncle Harold and Shirley were very happy. They decided to get married and live together above Shirley's shop.

But Harold took so long getting
ready that he almost missed the
wedding.

He didn't want to go on honeymoon. He thought the sun would be bad for his hair and the seaweed would get caught in his beard.

Shirley began to get cross. She liked
to go dancing in the evenings but
Harold always had to stay in and
wash his hair.

When Shirley saw Harold looking
in the mirror and saying, "Hello,
Harold, you lovely big hairy man,"
she began to get jealous.

She thought that Harold must love
his hair more than he loved her.
So Shirley did a terrible thing. The
worst thing that anyone can do to
a hairy man.

When Harold was asleep, she took
her hairdressing scissors and snipped
off his beautiful hair.

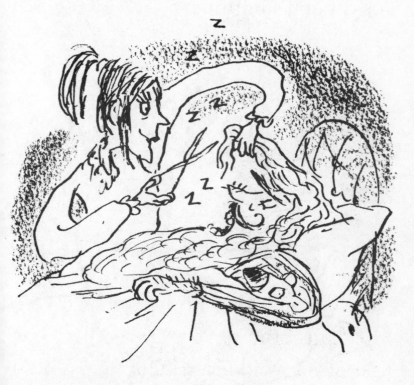

Then she chopped off his big
bushy beard.

Then Shirley took her hairdresser's
shaver and shaved Harold from
head to foot until he was as smooth
as a baby's bottom.

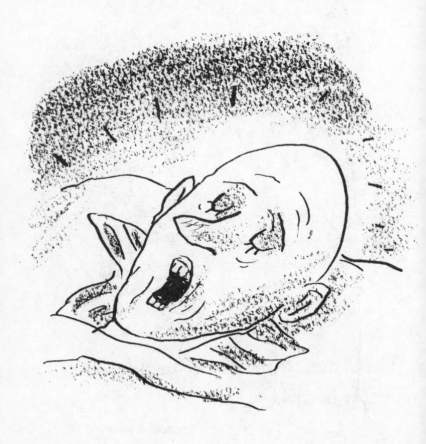

When Uncle Harold woke up
he went to the mirror. He said,
"Hello, Harold, you lovely big...

AAARRRGGGH!"

Then poor Uncle Harold began
to cry. "Someone has stolen
my beautiful hair," he sobbed.
"Someone has stolen my
beautiful hair."

Harold went downstairs to Shirley's shop in his pyjamas. Everybody stared at him. Shirley went over to Harold and kissed his bald head.

Then everyone in the shop said,
"We want to be bald too. Just
like Harold."

Uncle Harold looked at himself in all the mirrors. Then he began to smile. He stroked his smooth bald head. "Hello, Harold, you lovely big bald man," he said.

THE END

My FREAKY FAMILY

COLLECT THEM ALL!

Also available as an ebook